Mermaid School

Ready, Steady, Swim!

The
Mermaid
School
Series

Mermaid School
The Clamshell Show
Ready, Steady, Swim!

Look out for more in the series—coming soon!

Mermaid School

Ready, Steady, Swim!

Written by
Lucy Courtenay

Illustrated by Sheena Dempsey

Amulet Books
New York

Cataloging-in-Publication Data has been applied for and may be obtained from the Library of Congress.

Hardcover ISBN 978-1-4197-4522-5
Paperback ISBN 978-1-4197-4523-2

Text copyright © 2020 Lucy Courtenay
Illustrations copyright © 2020 Sheena Dempsey

Printed and bound in U.S.A.
10 9 8 7 6 5 4 3 2 1

Amulet Books are available at special discounts when purchased in quantity for premiums and promotions as well as fundraising or educational use. Special editions can also be created to specification. For details, contact specialsales@abramsbooks.com or the address below.

Amulet Books® is a registered trademark of Harry N. Abrams, Inc.

ABRAMS The Art of Books
195 Broadway, New York, NY 10007
abramsbooks.com

Chapter One

Marnie Blue had never seen such a huge scary merman. His black beard covered his enormous chest. The blue light of the Sports Cave rippled over his arm tattoos.

"TRAINED TO AQUA-OLYMPIC LEVEL, OF COURSE . . ." he was saying very loudly to Ms. Mullet, the crab deputy head of Lady Sealia Foam's Mermaid School, as Marnie and her friends swam into the Sports Cave for their PE lesson.

"Who is THAT?" Marnie asked.

"Well, he's not Miss Haddock," said Pearl Cockle.

He certainly wasn't Miss Haddock, their usual PE teacher.

Miss Haddock was old and nearsighted and didn't approve of tattoos. She had been the fishball champion of Mermaid Lagoon in her youth, but that wasn't saying much. Fishball was the most boring sport Marnie had ever played. It had lots of rules and hardly any swimming around. This merman looked like he would eat Miss Haddock for lunch.

Ms. Mullet looked even smaller than usual next to the giant visitor. "Good morning, class," she said. "I'm sorry to say that Miss Haddock had an accident last night and won't be with us today."

Dora Agua gasped. "Is Miss Haddock all right, Ms. Mullet?"

"Miss Haddock mistook a reef shark for her pet catfish," Ms. Mullet said. "She is expected to make a full recovery, but she will be in hospital for a while."

Most of the mermaids were fond of Miss Haddock, because she never made them swim around too fast and sometimes brought her catfish, Cecil, to lessons.

Others were less concerned.

"I hope Miss Haddock retires after this," said Gilly Seaflower. "Her lessons are really boring."

"That's a terrible thing to say, Gilly," snapped Orla Finnegan. "How would YOU like to be eaten by a shark?"

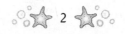

"If she was **EATEN**, she'd be dead," Gilly pointed out as she tied back her long blonde curls with a seaweed hairband. "I bet she was only nibbled. She's a silly old trout and I won't miss her."

Marnie frowned. Gilly could be really mean sometimes.

"This guy looks like he might actually teach us something, though," Lupita Barracuda said thoughtfully.

Lupita was a member of the local speed-swimming club, and was always team captain in Miss Haddock's lessons. She also had the most flexible tail Marnie had ever seen and could do ten backflips in a row. Marnie could understand her interest in the new teacher. Marnie, on the other hand, was worried. She wasn't very sporty.

Ms. Mullet clacked her deep-red pincers to get everyone's attention.

"This is Mr. Marlin," she said. "He comes from Lord Foam's Atoll Academy with excellent references. I am happy to leave you in his capable fins."

She swam away in her usual sideways fashion.

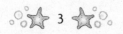

3

Mr. Marlin frowned at the class. "Hmm," he said.

"Good morning, Mr. Marlin," said the class cautiously.

There was a pair of pretty ladies tattooed on the new PE teacher's arms. He flexed his muscles, making the ladies bounce around. *Miss Haddock would* definitely *not approve of those,* Marnie thought.

"TEN LAPS OF THE SPORTS CAVE," Mr. Marlin suddenly screamed, making Marnie jump. "GET THOSE FLABBY FINS MOVIIIIIIING!"

4

Half the class shot forward in a blur of brightly-colored tails. The rest followed more slowly. Marnie stayed beside Orla and Pearl in the middle of the pack. Lupita's gleaming black tail was streaking ahead of everyone else. Gilly wasn't far behind.

"MY GRANDMOTHER CAN SWIM FASTER THAN YOU!" Mr. Marlin shrieked. "AND SHE'S A HUNDRED AND THREE!"

Pearl was smaller than the rest of the class, and now her little tail was struggling to keep up. Marnie and Orla slowed down to keep her company.

"NO SLACKING AT THE BACK!" screeched Mr. Marlin.

Soon, Marnie had a pain in her side. Pearl's glasses were misting up with the effort. Orla's pale face was almost as purple as her tail. Lupita overtook them on the next lap, shooting them a grin over her shoulder.

"Move your tails, sea snails!" whooped Gilly, following close behind Lupita.

Round and round they went. Marnie lost count of the number of times they swam past the old fishball nets. She just wanted it to end.

Finally, it did. Lupita won, of course. Marnie and her friends collapsed to the floor of the Sports Cave, groaning.

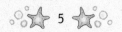 5

"You!" said Mr. Marlin, pointing at Lupita. "Very good."

Marnie clapped. So did a few others. Lupita was really popular.

"You!" Mr. Marlin pointed at Gilly, who had come second. "Useless."

A few people giggled. Gilly turned bright red with humiliation.

"If you're not first, you lose," said Mr. Marlin. "WINNING is the most important thing."

"I *nearly* won, Mr. Marlin!" Gilly's lip wobbled. "I was only half a tail behind Lupita. I—"

"Make like a sardine and *can it*," said Mr. Marlin. "I only want WINNERS in my class." He glared at everyone else who lay sprawled and wheezing on the rocky floor. "FIVE MORE LAPS FOR EVERYONE EXCEPT TODAY'S WINNER."

The class groaned.

"Can I do five more laps anyway, sir?" asked Lupita.

"Excellent attitude," said Mr. Marlin. "The rest of you could learn a thing or two from this pupil. Now off you go. What are you waiting for?"

"I thought torture was against the law." Orla grumbled as the class swam around the Sports Cave all over again.

"My tail is going to fall off," groaned Pearl.

Marnie's own tail felt like it was stuffed with rocks. She held out her hand. "We'll do it together," she suggested.

Pearl took Marnie's hand gratefully. "Thanks, Marnie."

"FASTER!" Mr. Marlin screeched. "YOU'RE SLACKER THAN MY GRANDMOTHER'S FISHING LINE AND IT'S EVEN OLDER THAN SHE IS!"

Chapter Two

"I'm going to complain to Lady Sealia," said Orla as they sat in the Galloping Scallop café that afternoon, slurping sea-foam smoothies and trying not to think about how much they ached all over. "Mermaids aren't meant to swim that fast. We're meant to sit around and brush our hair and sing."

"And become marine biologists like my mom," said Pearl. "And hydro-engineers. And—"

"Well, obviously all those things too," said Orla. "But when was the last time you saw a marine biologist racing about like there's pins in her fins?"

Marnie put down her salted sea-urchin cookie. "It's about fitness, I guess," she said. "If you're healthy, you can do your job better. If you're healthy, you can sing for longer because your lungs are superstrong."

Orla grunted and took another slurp of her smoothie. "Well, I think it's stupid."

Marnie glanced over to where Lupita was sitting with Dora. Lupita's cheeks were flushed and her eyes sparkled as she laughed at something Dora was saying. Across the café, Gilly was deep in conversation with Mabel. She had been very quiet after PE, which was kind of a nice change.

"So what do you think of this place?" Pearl said, jolting Marnie out of her thoughts.

"The cookies are good," Marnie said. "Did your dad make them?"

"He made everything on the menu," said Pearl proudly.

Pearl's dad had just opened the café to go alongside his fish-farming business. The fish was the freshest in Mermaid Lagoon, and the cookie flavors were surprising

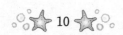 10

and delicious. Judging from how busy it was, the Galloping Scallop was going to be a swim-away success. Half of Lady Sealia's was here, chatting and joking over sea-foam smoothies and cookies. Several merboys from Atoll Academy were in a large, brightly colored coral booth at the back of the café. Marnie recognized Eddy and Algie, who had performed with them in the recent Clamshell Show. The booth had been empty when Marnie and her friends arrived, but Pearl was allergic to coral, so they had chosen a table by the window.

Orla glanced across the café at the merboys. "Didn't Ms. Mullet say Mr. Marlin came from Atoll Academy?"

When Marnie nodded, Orla leaned back in her seat. "Hey, Eddy," she shouted across the café to a merboy with brown hair and a cheeky smile. "What's Mr. Marlin like?"

Gilly and Mabel started giggling and tossing their hair around. Marnie rolled her eyes.

"Snarlin' Marlin?" said Eddy. "He's a nightmare. He made Lord Foam *cry* once."

Lord Foam was Lady Sealia's husband, and almost as big as Mr. Marlin. Marnie couldn't imagine anyone making the big, red-bearded head of Atoll Academy cry.

"He's our new PE teacher," said Orla, rather glumly.

Eddy looked sympathetic. "Try not to come last in anything," he said.

Gilly gave a squeal of silly laughter, flicked her hair and fell off her café chair.

"You're very quiet tonight, Marnie," said Marnie's mom. "Is everything all right?"

Marnie's aunt Christabel put down her sparkly nail polish and leaned her elbows on the table. "Leave the girl alone, Daffy," she said. "She's probably thinking about a *merboy*."

"I'm not!" Marnie said indignantly.

"Prove it then," Aunt Christabel challenged. "Tell us what's on your mind."

Garbo, Aunt Christabel's pet goldfish, snuck the nail polish bottle off the table and took it to her bowl in the corner of the room. Garbo loved sparkly things. And as the most famous singer and radio star in Mermaid Lagoon, Aunt Christabel had a LOT of sparkly things.

Marnie sighed. "There's this new PE teacher," she said.

"Has Miss Haddock retired?" asked Marnie's mom.

"It's about time," said Christabel. "She was ancient even when WE were at school."

Marnie explained about Miss Haddock's accident, and Snarlin' Marlin, and what the merboys had been saying about him.

"He must know what he's doing," said Marnie's mom, doubtfully. "Or Lady Sealia wouldn't have given him the job."

"Marlin, did you say?" asked Christabel. "We had a message at Radio SeaWave yesterday from a Mr. Marlin, asking me to present the prizes at a big school sports event. I thought he meant Atoll Academy. Lady Sealia doesn't really go in for that sort of thing."

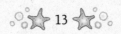

A big school sports event? Marnie's heart lurched. It was just the sort of thing Mr. Marlin would organize.

"And even if she did," Christabel was saying, "I'd be the last mermaid in the lagoon who Lady Sealia would want to present the prizes."

"You ARE the most famous mermaid in the lagoon," her mom pointed out. "It must mean Lady Sealia has forgiven you for that . . . *incident* at the Clamshell Show."

"You mean my long-lost human sweetheart turning up and terrifying the scales off everyone?" Christabel said. "I don't think Lady Sealia has forgiven me for that at ALL."

Christabel hadn't mentioned Arthur, her old sweetheart, since the Clamshell Show disaster, when Lady Sealia had banished him from the lagoon and threatened to have sea monsters eat him if he ever came back. Marnie was surprised to hear Christabel mention him now. She wondered if her aunt was missing him.

"We used to have an annual sports tournament when we were at school," said Marnie's mom, quickly changing the subject. "Do you remember, Chrissie?"

"Garbo, bring my nail polish **BACK**," Christabel ordered, finally noticing it had gone missing. "I didn't really do sports at school, Daffy."

"But you must remember Golden Glory Day!" her mom said. Her blue eyes grew dreamy. "The fishball tournament, the prizes, the Crown!"

Christabel shuddered. "Fishball is a horrible game. Your fingernails get so slimy."

"It was a big event," Daphne told Marnie. "The Golden Glory Crown was presented to the winner. But they canceled it in our final year. Such a shame."

Marnie had never heard of Golden Glory Day. "Why did they cancel it?"

Marnie's mom sighed. "Because the Golden Glory Crown disappeared." Christabel dropped the nail polish she'd just retrieved from Garbo. Garbo gleefully snatched it up again, and swam off into a dark corner with her prize.

"What was the Crown like?" Marnie asked, entranced.

"It was made of gold and coral and diamonds and all the usual things that turn up on the lagoon bed," Marnie's mom said vaguely. She wasn't that interested in fashion. "It belonged to Queen Maretta herself, you know. And there was something *extra* special about it . . ."

Christabel rose from the table to collect the plates. "This is all ancient history. I'm sure Marnie doesn't want to hear it."

"Oh, but I do!" said Marnie eagerly. She loved hearing anything about Maretta, the most famous queen of Mermaid Lagoon. "What was so special about the Crown?"

"It granted a wish," said Marnie's mom. "But only a true winner of the Crown could make the wish, so it was of no use to an ordinary thief. I never understood why anyone would steal it. It was nice and sparkly of course, but that doesn't seem like a good reason to steal something—"

"Marnie, help me to catch Garbo, will you?" interrupted Christabel. "I've still got three nails to paint. Come here, you naughty little beast, or I will put you in a goldfish stew!"

Marnie thought there was something sad in her aunt's eyes as she helped Christabel to chase Garbo around the room. She was about to ask her if she was feeling all right, when Christabel snatched up the nail polish, tucked it into her pocket, and clapped her hands.

"Enough talk about silly sports," she said briskly. "It's not winning that counts, Marnie, no matter what this new PE teacher says. It's not even participating. It's the not being caught for not participating. I was always pretty good at that."

Chapter Three

Marnie was late the next day. Garbo had stolen her favorite sparkly shell pen and it had taken forever to find it. And then her tail had been so stiff and achy from Mr. Marlin's PE lesson that she could only swim extremely slowly. By the time she reached Lady Sealia's, the whole school was in an assembly. Marnie swam as quietly as she could into the big, pale blue cave and joined her friends at the back.

"And so in three weeks, our first years will be competing in the new Golden Glory Day," Lady Sealia was saying, her long white hair piled regally on top of her head. Her pet dogfish, Dilys, was in her arms, snoozing as usual. "The rest of the school will, of course, be invited to the festivities. It is going to be a marvelous occasion, and we should all thank Mr. Marlin for organizing it at such short notice."

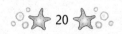

The new PE teacher was swimming up and down the aisles, glaring. His black beard rippled like the tentacles of an angry squid.

"Golden Glory Day?" Marnie said as everyone around her clapped politely. "Mom was telling me about Golden Glory Day last night. They used to award the Golden Glory Crown to the winner, but then it went missing."

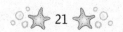

"Lady Sealia mentioned some crown just before you swam in," said Orla. "It sounds like no one knows where it is anymore."

"Well, guess what?" said Marnie. "The Crown grants a WISH."

Pearl looked interested. "What kind of wish?"

"Anything, I think," Marnie said. She couldn't quite remember the details.

"And it's missing?" said Orla.

"QUIET AT THE BACK, YOU SNIVELING SPRATS!" screamed Mr. Marlin.

Miss Tangle, the octopus music teacher, jumped in fright and got her arms in a tangle, trying to pick up the glasses which had fallen off.

"Thank you, Mr. Marlin," said Lady Sealia. "We will put our first years into new school teams for the occasion: Whitecaps, Billows, Breakers, and Ripples. These teams will be decided during your next PE class."

"Tell us about the missing crown, Marnie," said Orla eagerly. "Does it only grant one wish? Where do you think it is? Did someone steal it? Maybe we could try and find it! We—"

"Shh!" said Marnie, her eyes fixed on Mr. Marlin as he prowled up and down.

Lady Sealia peered vaguely around the room. She was rather nearsighted, but too vain to wear her glasses. "We will have three events," she said. "Ultra Fishball, Obstacle Relay, and Seahorse Racing."

The cave burst into chatter.

"Ultra fishball!" said Lupita in wonder. "Ultra fishball is a really cool update on the old game. It's much faster than the way that old crabstick Miss Haddock teaches it. There's actual speed-swimming, and full contact, and—"

"THE NEXT PERSON TO SPEAK WILL DO A HUNDRED PULL-UPS!" shrieked Mr. Marlin.

The cave fell quiet again. The only sound was a sleepy sneeze from Dilys.

"There will also be a special Golden Glory Day cheerleading squad, open to all members of the school," Lady Sealia said, stroking Dilys's fins. "Miss Tangle will be holding practices every lunchtime for the next three weeks. Just go along to the Music Cave if you would like to join."

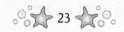

Marnie sat up. *That* was more like it. She had one of the best voices in Mermaid School, and she loved performing. She pictured dancing and waving sea-anemone pom-poms and turning awesome somersaults as the crowds cheered and clapped. Suddenly, the thought of Golden Glory Day wasn't so bad after all.

"You're going to do the cheerleading, right?" she asked Orla.

"Hmm?" said Orla, with a faraway look on her face. Marnie guessed she was thinking about the Crown, and the magic wish. "Oh! Yes. Cheerleading all the way, stingray."

"I'm not good at sports *or* singing," Pearl said, rather gloomily. "Unless they have a fish-spotting competition, I don't think I'm going to enjoy Golden Glory Day."

"What's the prize, Lady Sealia?" someone called out. "Since the Crown is missing?"

"The prize will be the honor of winning," said Lady Sealia, rather severely.

"A magic crown would definitely be better," Orla whispered to Marnie.

"And finally, I'm pleased to say that we will have a very special guest with us," Lady Sealia went on. "Mermaid Lagoon's most famous radio star, Christabel Blue, has agreed to bring Radio SeaWave to our event. She will broadcast during the day and present the prize to the winning team."

The headteacher didn't look nearly as thrilled about this as Mr. Marlin. Something told Marnie that the PE teacher had invited Christabel without asking Lady Sealia first.

There was a cheer. Marnie enjoyed the rush of pride she always felt for Aunt Christabel. A few mermaids craned their necks to look at Marnie, and whispered behind their hands. Marnie didn't like that part so much.

"Is your aunt really bringing her show to Golden Glory Day, Marnie?" Dora Agua asked as they swam to their first lesson of the day. "That is off the *reef*! Will she do shout-outs for all the first years?"

"Christabel Blue must be desperate if she's doing her show at a dumb school sports day," said Gilly Seaflower as she swam past Marnie and her friends. "Her career has really taken a dive."

"Oh go fall off a café chair, Gilly," said Orla.

Gilly flushed and swam away quickly, with her friends trailing in her wake.

"That girl is such a pain," Orla said. "If *I* find the Golden Glory Crown, I'm going to make a wish to send her and all her friends to the Arctic Ocean."

"If I find the Golden Glory Crown, I'll wish for a colony of giant spotted sailfish to come and live in Mermaid Lagoon," Pearl said dreamily.

"You are so weird," said Orla.

Marnie wondered what she'd wish for. She wanted some new pearl earrings, but that felt a bit boring. So did a lifetime's supply of tail polish. She tried to remember more details about the Crown. Her mom had mentioned something about the wish, but she couldn't remember what it was.

"A magic wish should be used for something really important," she said out loud. She was sure about that at least. "Something that could change your life."

"Like getting rid of Gilly Seaflower," said Orla.

"Like giant spotted sailfish," Pearl said at the same time.

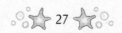

"First cheerleading session this lunchtime, girls," Miss Tangle said, sailing past in a tangle of arms. "We're going to put on a routine that would impress Queen Maretta herself! Don't forget!"

Chapter Four

The next PE class came around too soon.

"I've been thinking about the missing Golden Glory Crown," Orla said as they swam reluctantly to the Sports Cave.

Thinking about the Crown was more fun than worrying about PE. Marnie felt a little more cheerful. "What about it?" she said.

"I think it's here." Orla opened her arms, and waved at the rocky corridor. "In the school."

"But they must have searched the school when it went missing," Pearl pointed out, pushing her glasses up her freckled nose.

"Exactly!" Orla said. "Whenever I lose something, Mom tells me to look in the place where I last saw it. And it's **ALWAYS** there, even though I looked really hard the first time."

"But what if someone stole it and took it away from school and sold it?" Marnie said.

Orla shook her head firmly. "It's here. I can feel its *golden magic presence*."

Marnie felt a little shiver of excitement when Orla said that.

"So I think we should start looking for it," Orla continued. "We'll start at lunchtime."

"But we have cheerleading practice at lunch," Marnie pointed out.

"After school then," said Orla. "Who's with me?"

"Me!" Marnie said at once.

"Me too!" said Pearl.

Marnie and her friends zoomed into the Sports Cave, all feeling lighter at the thought of a treasure hunt after school. Lupita was already there, swishing her gleaming black tail and telling the other mermaids about an ultra fishball match she had seen.

"The Flying Flounders were totally *smashing* the Raving Rays and there was this massive crash by the fishball goal and someone actually broke their *arm* and no one even APOLOGIZED. It was turtley awesome!"

Marnie was shocked. Miss Haddock had always taught the mermaids that good manners on the fishball court were more important than winning the game. Fishball lessons had always been full of "Sorry" and "Pardon me." Her mood dipped again.

"I wonder which teams we'll be on?" said Pearl.

"I hope we're in the same one," said Orla.

"Oh!" Marnie said in horror. "But we *have* to be in the same team! I can't do an obstacle relay or ultra fishball or seahorse racing without you guys! How can we make sure we're together?"

"Easy," Pearl said. "Make sure we're four mermaids apart when Mr. Marlin makes us line up. He'll just go one, two, three, four down the line. That's what teachers always do."

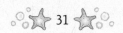

Above their heads, Mr. Marlin was doing pull-ups from a jutting part of the cave roof. He let go and dropped with impressive speed to the Sports Cave floor. He had braided his long black beard, and it looked a bit silly flying up over his shoulder.

"**LINE UP, YOU SOPPY SEAWORMS,**" he roared.

Marnie counted carefully and squeezed into the line next to Gilly. Gilly looked surprised, and gave her a dirty look. For a moment, Marnie worried that Mr. Marlin would just group them into teams depending on who they were next to.

"There are twenty-four of you, so that will be six members to each team," Mr. Marlin began. "One, two, three, FOUR, one, two, three, FOUR . . ."

Mr. Marlin swam down the jostling line, counting heads. Gilly was a three, and Marnie was a four. One or two mermaids realized what was happening, and tried to swim away from their friends. But it was too late.

"If I said ONE, you're Team Whitecaps," said Mr. Marlin, folding his massive arms. "TWO: Team Billows. THREE: Team Breakers. FOUR: Team Ripples. No exceptions. Get into your teams NOW!"

Four meant Marnie was on Team Ripples. Her heart beat fast as she swam out of the line, looking for her friends. Orla and Pearl were next to the fishball nets, grinning and waving at her, along with Kerri Kelp-Matthews, Allira Bladder, and Ripley van der Zee.

"Neptune's knickers, I thought I was on Gilly's team for sure," said Orla.

"Works every time," Pearl said happily.

Lupita was Team Whitecaps with some of the sportier students, including Mintie Spratt, who had the size and strength of a giant squid, and super-bendy Cordelia Glitter, who could tie her own tail in a knot. Dora had made the mistake of staying next to Lupita, and was floating gloomily in Team Billows with Mabel Anemone, Nerida Attwater, Treasure Jones, and the bickering Fysshe-Fynne twins, who hated each other and had tried to stay as far apart as possible. Gilly Seaflower was Team Breakers. From the way she was waving her arms at timid Finnula Gritt and dreamy Zarya Sand-Smith, Gilly was already taking charge.

"Team Whitecaps is definitely going to win," said Kerri Kelp-Matthews gloomily.

"I wish we'd got a cooler-sounding team," Orla said. "Team Ripples sounds like it's never going to win anything."

"It's not the winning that matters," said Marnie.

"OH YES IT IS," said Mr. Marlin, who had overheard. "Swim to the roof of the cave and back five times. GO!"

Miss Tangle drummed her tentacles on her music stand. The cheerleading group was trying to pin down some lyrics for a song to inspire the four teams for Golden Glory Day. And it wasn't going well.

"What's the matter with you?" she demanded, peering through her glasses. "Not one of you is singing in tune."

"We're a bit out of breath, Miss Tangle," said Marnie, whose tummy ached. "PE lesson."

Ultra fishball had been exhausting. The school flatfish weren't used to being thrown so hard and had started misbehaving. By the end of the lesson, Marnie's hands were covered in so much fish slime that she could hardly see her fingernails.

Miss Tangle looked unimpressed. "I need *inspiration*, not perspiration. Now from the top, middle, and bottom!"

"*Whitecaps surge with sea-foam bright*," Marnie sang, doing her best not to let her voice wobble.

"Billows roll with all their might,
Breakers drive against the gales,
Ripples..."

That's where the song stopped.

Miss Tangle lifted her tentacles to the roof. "Come to me, Inspiration!" she said, rather dramatically. *"Ripples ... Ripples ..."*

"All have smelly scales?" offered Gilly with a snicker.

Other unhelpful suggestions included *"are the size of whales"* and *"are a bunch of fails."* Orla looked like she was about to explode. Marnie was too tired to think of anything.

"How about *'Watching Breakers is a treat, Ripples are the ones to beat'*?" Pearl suggested. Pearl wasn't a singer, but she had come along to the practice to support Marnie and Orla.

Miss Tangle flung out her tentacles in delight. It made her look like a starfish. "Perfect!" she cried.

There were a few mutters. Gilly, Zarya, Finnula, and the other mermaids in Breakers had liked the line about gales.

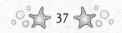

"Once more from the top, middle, and bottom!" Miss Tangle trilled.

"*Whitecaps surge with sea-foam bright*," sang Marnie, holding hands with Pearl on one side and Orla on the other.

"Billows roll with all their might;
Watching Breakers is a treat,
Ripples are the ones to beat.
Lady Sealia's wins the day,
Lady Sealia's, hip hooray!
Lady Sealia's wins the day,
 Lady Sealia's—hip, hip, HOORAY!"

Chapter
Five

"*Whitecaps surge with sea-foam bright, la, la, la . . .*" Marnie hummed the catchy little cheerleading tune the whole way through oceanography.

"Who is 'umming?" demanded Mr. Scampi, the large black lobster who taught oceanography. "Stop! We cannot concentrate on our coral samples."

Pearl sneezed sadly. She loved oceanography, but she had forgotten to take her allergy medicine that morning and her eyes were so red and puffy from the coral that she could hardly see what she was doing. Marnie passed her a seaweed handkerchief and tried her best to stop humming.

The magical Golden Glory Crown shimmered in her mind like a beautiful sparkly dream. If they found it, they would be heroes. She couldn't wait for the lesson to end so that they could start their treasure hunt.

Finally it *was* over and they could leave once they'd cleared away their samples. "I never want to hear about coral again," said Orla. "Polyps *this* and polyps *that*. It's like Mr. Scampi was doing it on **PURPOSE**."

Pearl blew her nose so loudly that a nearby scallop clattered into the rocky wall. "Teaching us about coral polyps is Mr. Scampi's job," she pointed out.

"But finding the Golden Glory Crown is **MUCH** more important," said Orla impatiently. "If we find it, you could wish for all the oceanography knowledge in the whole world. You'd never need to go to another oceanography class in your life."

Marnie had meant to ask her mom how the wish worked last night. There was something about the Crown that she had forgotten . . .

"Where shall we start looking?" said Pearl.

"Lady Sealia's office," Orla said immediately.

Marnie blinked. The only time she'd ever been in Lady Sealia's office was when she was in trouble.

"Think about it," said Orla. "Where's the LAST place you'd look for it? Right under Lady Sealia's nose, of course."

Marnie and Pearl looked at each other. This didn't sound like a good idea at all.

"Wait, Orla—" Marnie tried, but Orla had already swum away down the corridor.

There was nothing else to do. They followed her.

Lady Sealia's door was closed.

"What's the plan?" said Pearl, looking at Marnie.

"I don't HAVE a plan," Marnie said. She felt as if a shoal of clownfish was doing somersaults in her tummy. "This wasn't my idea!"

"Let's just knock and see what happens," said Orla confidently.

She raised her fist and banged on Lady Sealia's door.

To everyone's surprise, the door swung open. Dilys, Lady Sealia's pet dogfish, slowly raised her head from her sea-moss cushion and peered down her long snout at them. There was no sign of the headteacher.

"Lady Sealia must have forgotten to shut the door properly," Pearl guessed.

Orla clapped her hands. "Perfect! We can search the office before she gets back."

"I don't think we should be in here, Orla," said Marnie anxiously.

"Marnie's right," Pearl said, hovering by the door. "We'll get in a lot of trouble."

"And when we find the Crown, we can simply wish ourselves OUT of trouble," Orla said. "Pearl, keep watch. I'll start with Lady Sealia's desk. Marnie, check out that big cupboard over there."

There was a snarling noise. Dilys was growling from her corner, her lips curled back from her sharp little teeth.

Marnie gulped. "Dilys doesn't want us in here."

"She's just a dopey dogfish," Orla said, peering under Lady Sealia's desk. "When have you seen her do anything except sleep? Ignore her."

"A dogfish is a kind of shark," Pearl pointed out from the doorway. "And sharks can be unpredictable. Just ask Miss Haddock."

Orla put her hands on her hips. "Do you want to find the Crown or not?"

For a dopey dogfish, Dilys was unbelievably fast. In a flash of silver-grey, she darted off her cushion and shot toward the door. Marnie jumped out of the way in case the little dogfish bit her. So did Pearl. With a flick of her long tail, Dilys escaped into the corridor—and vanished from sight.

There was a long and nasty silence.

"She'll come back," said Orla.

They waited.

"She's not coming back," Pearl moaned.

"I knew we shouldn't have gone into Lady Sealia's office, I knew it!" Marnie burst out. "And now Dilys has swum away and Lady Sealia is going to be so MAD!"

Marnie, Orla and Pearl rushed out of the office and down the corridor, calling the little dogfish's name. "Dilys! DILYS!"

Marnie was swimming so fast that she almost smacked into someone coming around the corner. Someone tall, and regal, with long white hair and a silver-white tail. Someone holding a little dogfish, who had gone back to sleep already.

"It is very unseemly for mermaids to rush about in this manner, Marnie Blue," said Lady Sealia. "You could have injured Dilys." She frowned down at the dogfish curled in her arms. "How did she escape from my office?"

Marnie swallowed. "Um," she began.

"Your door was open, Lady Sealia," said Orla, swimming to Marnie's rescue. "We knocked and you weren't there but your door opened and then . . . Dilys swam away."

It wasn't the whole truth, but it wasn't a lie either. Lady Sealia stroked Dilys behind her fins.

"Why did you knock on my door?" she said.

"It doesn't matter now," said Marnie quickly. She grabbed her friends' hands to drag them away. "Sorry Lady Sealia. We're glad Dilys is OK. Bye."

"That," said Pearl, when they were a safe distance from Lady Sealia, "was close."

"And very annoying," Orla grumbled. "We'll have to try again— OH!"

She suddenly pointed at something. Something perched on a ledge in the corridor wall. Something round, and spiky-looking.

"The Crown!" Orla cried.

Pearl frowned. "Wait—"

Orla beat her tail and shot up the corridor wall. "I found it!" she shouted, waving her arms. "Thrills and gills, I found the Crown!" Lifting it in the air, she looked triumphantly down at Marnie and Pearl. "I'm going to make the BEST wish—"

"No Orla, put it down!" said Pearl suddenly. "It's not the Crown, it's a venomous—"

But Orla had already put it on her head. She opened her mouth in surprise.

"*Ow*," she said faintly and fell to the floor.

Marnie clapped her hands to her mouth.

"—starfish," Pearl finished unhappily.

Chapter Six

Orla lay on the ground with some nasty, puffy lumps on her forehead. The starfish shot away down the corridor, angrily waggling its spines.

"We have to get Orla to the First Aid Cave," said Marnie, feeling frightened. She wished they'd never started looking for the Crown. "Help me, Pearl!"

With Marnie at Orla's head and Pearl holding her limp purple tail, they swam unsteadily up the corridor.

"Ow," Orla said again, woozily.

"You're going to be fine," Marnie said. She hoped it was true.

"I don't think it's a deadly one," said Pearl. "But I'm not very good on starfish identification."

Marnie wiped her face. Orla was heavy, and she was already tired from that day's PE class. They almost fell through the door of the First Aid Cave.

The First Aid Cave was a neat little cavern beside the Oceanography room. There were bottles of medicine on driftwood shelves and rolls of seaweed bandages tucked into rocky niches. Posters lined the walls, saying things like **TAIL ROT: DON'T SUFFER IN SILENCE** and **THE FIVE SIGNS OF FISH FLU.** A very large nurse shark almost filled the little space. As she turned around, her tail brushed the shelves and made the bottles of medicine shiver in their little bottles. She looked at Marnie and Orla with small, kind eyes.

"Oh dearie me," said Nurse Nurse-Shark. "What happened here?"

"Our friend put a starfish on her head by mistake," Marnie explained with a gulp. "Is she going to be all right?"

Nurse Nurse-Shark peered at the stings on Orla's head. "Painful, but not dangerous," she said. "Put her on the bed. I have an antidote somewhere, let me see..."

It was amazing to watch such a large shark swimming so delicately among the tiny bottles that lined the driftwood shelves. When her dorsal fin brushed the old chandelier on the ceiling, Marnie heard a faint jingle.

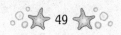

TAIL ROT
Don't Suffer
in
Silence

FIVE SIGNS
of
FISH FLU

Cod
Liver
Oil

"She can stay here for a few days," said Nurse Nurse-Shark, swimming back down with a small bottle. "She's had a nasty shock."

"But she'll be OK, won't she?" Marnie asked.

"She'll be fine. But perhaps in future, she should not wear an unidentified starfish as a hat?"

"I don't think the Crown is here at all," said Pearl as they swam into school together the next day. "I think someone stole it and it's long gone."

Marnie had finally asked her mom to explain the rules of the wish again. She felt even worse about Orla's stings now. "Do you think there's time to visit Orla before lessons?" she said. "I want to explain something. You'll want to hear it too, Pearl."

With her parents' rather anxious insistence, Orla had stayed overnight in case of complications from the starfish sting. When Pearl and Marnie arrived at the First Aid Cave, she was sitting up in bed scowling at herself in a little mirror.

"I'm covered in LUMPS," she said crossly.

"It was a crown-of-thorns starfish," said Pearl. "Of course you're covered in lumps."

Orla folded her arms. "It looked like *the* Crown. How was I supposed to know?"

"We're glad you're OK," said Marnie, squeezing her hand.

"We can keep looking when I get out of here," Orla said. "I've got some new ideas—"

"No," said Marnie firmly. "We're not looking any more. There's something I didn't tell you about the Crown, because I'd forgotten. It only grants a wish to the winner of Golden Glory Day. So even if we DID find it, the wish wouldn't even work."

Pearl looked disappointed. "Then Lupita will definitely win it. And she'll probably ask to keep Mr. Marlin forever."

Orla made a face. "Oh well," she said, staring around at the driftwood shelves and the old algae-covered chandelier. "At least I get to miss PE."

Mr. Marlin gathered the class outside School Rock later that day. "Obstacles," he announced. "We're doing this one in a relay. There can be no weak links."

They all gazed at the obstacle course before them. Marnie didn't like the slimy seaweed nets on the rocky lagoon bed, or the jagged coral spikes that would cut her tail if she swam too close. And she didn't even want to look at the dark, slimy tunnel beyond the nets. Moray eels lived in tunnels like that. Lupita and Cordelia clapped their hands with excitement. Gilly started doing push-ups. She wasn't very good at them, but Marnie had to admire her determination.

"I don't think I'll fit in that tunnel, sir," said Mintie Spratt.

"I was doing obstacle courses like this when I was no bigger than a tadpole," said Mr. Marlin. "If you can't get through it, then you're sea-weedier than I thought."

"Do you have any useful tips, Mr. Marlin?" said Gilly eagerly.

"Win," said the PE teacher with an evil smile. "And watch out for the jellyfish."

There were a few nervous titters of laughter. There was a jellyfish on the course? Marnie had never been stung by a jellyfish, but she'd heard that it hurt worse than anything.

"Oh," Mr. Marlin added, "and the last team to finish HAS TO DO IT AGAIN. Remember! If you don't come first, you LOSE. And no one remembers a LOSER. So plan your teams carefully."

"I'll go first," offered Allira as the teams gathered to discuss tactics. "Pearl, you take second. Orla's not here, so one of us will have to go twice. Who's the most athletic?"

They decided Kerri would go third and fifth, and Ripley fourth.

"Are you OK to go last, Marnie?" said Allira.

Marnie straightened her shoulders. "I'll do my best."

"First member of each team? Get set . . . GOLDFISH!" shouted Mr. Marlin. He put a whelk whistle to his lips and blew.

Kenda Wells was first for Whitecaps, Treasure Jones for Billows, and Fresca Brooke for Breakers. Marnie watched, holding her breath, as Kenda whisked ahead of the others, twisted through the coral spikes like an eel, darted under the nets, and vanished into the tunnel. Moments later there was a shout. She'd made it to the finish.

After a good start for Team Breakers, Marina Bailey refused to wriggle under the slimy nets, making Gilly snarl with frustration. Mintie Spratt got stuck in the tunnel, delaying Team Whitecaps by

several crucial starfish seconds. Pearl sneezed her way slowly through the coral, but Ripley van der Zee was surprisingly good at the net-crawling. The Fysshe-Fynne twins were arguing so loudly that they missed Nerida Attwater's triumphant finish, pushing Team Billows into last place. The gap between the teams closed again. The last four members of the teams—Marnie, Lupita, Dora, and Gilly—started together.

Marnie leapt toward the razor-sharp coral spikes, then

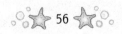

dove for the seaweed nets. The slime from the seaweed oozed through her hair. The gritty lagoon bed dug into her tummy. She scrambed out, panting.

"PUT YOUR TAILS INTO IT!" Mr. Marlin roared.

Marnie had fallen into a trough of gloopy sea-bed mud. The mud weighed her tail down, so she pulled herself along with her hands as best she could. Somewhere in the mud pool beside her, Dora was shrieking about her hair. Lupita was already out the other side.

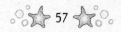

57

Now the tunnel loomed, dark and horrible. Marnie tried to spot the jellyfish Mr. Marlin had mentioned, but all she could see were strings of seaweed dangling over the tunnel mouth and two surprised-looking sea urchins.

"Get out of the way, LOSER!" Gilly barged past Marnie and into the tunnel.

Marnie was knocked off balance. She swam after Gilly as fast as she could, but she'd lost vital moments.

Inside the tunnel, it was even darker and slimier than she had thought. Eyes blinked at her from rocky crevices. Marnie kept her arms and fins as close to her body as she could.

There was a sudden squeal up ahead and a flash of light.

Marnie knew what it was at once.

The jellyfish had stung Gilly.

Chapter
Seven

"So how are you feeling?" Marnie asked, helping herself to one of the kelp cookies on Orla's bedside table. Nurse Nurse-Shark wasn't there, so they had the place to themselves.

"Much better," Orla said. "To be honest, I was feeling pretty good this morning. But I thought staying in bed would be more fun than PE."

"You were right," Marnie said. "There were these slimy nets, and all this mud . . . urgh. Oh, and Gilly was stung by a jellyfish Mr. Marlin had hidden in the tunnel."

"I know," said Orla. "She came in earlier. Her arm was bright red. What happened?"

"She pushed past me," said Marnie. She shivered. "If she hadn't, the jellyfish would have stung me instead."

"Gilly is taking this whole thing *way* too seriously," Orla said. "All she talks about is winning."

Marnie didn't want to think about Gilly. "If you're feeling better," she suggested, "why don't I teach you the stuff we learned in cheerleading practice today?"

Orla brightened. "Cool!"

Marnie showed her the moves. They swung their tails from side to side, and Orla copied Marnie's arm movements. They had to imagine the anemone pompoms, which Miss Tangle had promised to get for the next practice.

"Arms like THIS," instructed Marnie. "Tail like THAT. Swim straight UP. *Whitecaps surge with sea-foam bright, Billows roll with all their might . . .*"

Orla threw herself into the routine. The First Aid Cave was a bit too small for dramatic arm-waving, but they did their best.

> "*Watching Breakers is a treat,*
> *Ripples are the ones to beat.*
> *Lady Sealia's wins the day,*
> *Lady Sealia's, hip hooray!*
> *Lady Sealia's wins the day,*
> *Lady Sealia's—hip, hip,*
> **HOORAY!**"

On the last "HOORAY!" Marnie showed Orla the

complicated backwards somersault they were all going to do. Orla copied it a little too enthusiastically, and her tail crashed into the old chandelier on the ceiling of the cave, which shook and jingled. There was a funny flash of gold. Several little bottles were knocked off the top shelf and drifted gently to the floor.

"Oops," Orla said, giggling breathlessly. "Maybe I should save that somersault for outside."

They quickly collected the drifting bottles and put them back on the top shelf. Marnie glanced curiously at the old chandelier as it swayed and settled back into place. She'd probably imagined the golden flash. There was nothing golden about the chandelier's dark green, algae-covered branches.

Nurse Nurse-Shark swam into the cave just as they replaced the final bottle.

"I hope you are resting," she said to Orla.

"Yes, nurse," said Orla, hopping back into bed and pulling the covers up to her chin. "I'm still very ill."

"Hmm," said Nurse Nurse-Shark. "I think perhaps you can go back to your classes."

Orla coughed hopefully.

"Although not PE," added the nurse shark. "It might be wise to leave that a little longer."

Marnie shot her friend an envious glance. Lucky, *lucky* Orla.

"Jellyfish? Coral spikes?" said Aunt Christabel. She helped herself to sea-sponge pudding. "This PE teacher of yours sounds horrible. Let's arrange for an octopus to kidnap him."

Marnie relaxed a little. It was hard to stay anxious when her aunt said things like that.

"Well I think this new teacher is very good for your fitness," said Marnie's mom stoutly. "And I'm looking forward to the return of Golden Glory Day. It was always very *festive*."

"We've got to practice seahorse racing tomorrow," said Marnie.

"That's more like it," Aunt Christabel said. "Will you ride Urchin?"

Urchin was a bad-tempered school seahorse. Christabel had ridden him when she was at school, and he adored her. He adored Marnie too.

"I don't know," said Marnie. "Mr. Marlin wants to test us all. Then he'll choose the four best riders, one from each team."

"Urchin is the fastest seahorse in the school stable, and you're the only one who can ride him," Aunt Christabel pointed out. "Of course you'll be chosen."

Marnie loved Urchin, but the thought of competing on him was terrifying. "Maybe," she mumbled.

"I can't believe it'll be Golden Glory Day in just one week!" Marnie's mom exclaimed. "I'm going to make a new hat for the occasion."

Marnie sighed. Her mom had once made her an entire jacket out of mussel shells. Marnie had clanked dutifully about the lagoon frightening the fish for a few days, before accidentally-on-purpose losing it. Unlike Christabel, her mom's fashion sense was a bit . . . experimental.

"Neptune save us all!" muttered Christabel, grinning at Marnie.

But Marnie didn't grin back. Right now, her mom's new hat felt like the least of her worries.

As the mermaids gathered for their final Golden Glory Day preparations, the seahorses peeped over their oyster-shell half doors and snorted for attention. Marnie could feel Urchin's intense blue eyes on her.

"You will race three times around School Rock," Mr. Marlin shouted. "And then you will return to the starting line. Couldn't be simpler, even for a bunch of finny-ninnies like you. Mr. Splendid? We need your four fastest seahorses."

The toadfish stable master stroked his wide chin with one frilly yellow fin. "I have fast seahorses," Mr. Splendid said. "And I have seahorses you can ride. They are not the same thing."

"I want the fast ones," Mr. Marlin said. "This is a **RACE**. Not a picnic."

Mr. Splendid raised his eyebrows. "As you wish."

Urchin headed straight for Marnie, batting his little blue fins with excitement and nudging at her with his long bony nose. Two more—the golden-eyed Sandy and an enormous grey seahorse named Eric—floated quietly beside their stable doors. The fourth seahorse didn't come out of his stable at all.

"I said **FOUR**, Mr. Splendid," said Mr. Marlin. "Are you deaf?"

"Typhoon needs a little encouragement," Mr. Splendid said mildly.

"Encouragement? I'll give him encouragement," snorted Mr. Marlin. He flexed his arms and swam into the fourth stable. "Out you come, you lazy bag of fishbones—"

There was a shriek of rage, a flash of sharp teeth, and a thump. The **PE** teacher flew back out of the stable. His eyes were wide with shock. His beard resembled a spiny sea urchin. Marnie couldn't help giggling. No one *ever* rode Typhoon.

"You," Mr. Marlin shouted at Lupita, trying to smooth out his beard. The kick from Typhoon hadn't improved his temper. "Take the blue beast."

Urchin snapped at Lupita and pressed himself against Marnie. Marnie tried making encouraging noises, but he stayed where he was and glared at anyone else who tried to come close.

"Looks like you're representing Ripples, girlie," Mr. Marlin said.

Gilly got Tigershark, a speedy brown seahorse with very large teeth that stuck out like the prow of a ship. Mabel Anemone was on Sandy. Lupita ended up perched high on Eric. Marnie sighed and mounted Urchin.

"Let's just do our best," she whispered in his ear.

"Everybody line up," shouted Mr. Marlin.

Marnie glanced at the other riders. Lupita was braiding her curly hair out of her face, balancing perfectly on Eric's huge grey back. Mabel looked as wobbly as a blobfish. Gilly's eyes were blazing with determination. She held Tigershark's reins so tightly that the brown seahorse was shaking his head angrily at the bit between his protruding teeth.

"And . . . GO!"

Marnie knew Urchin would never hurt her on purpose, but the jagged edges of School Rock looked pretty scary when you were flying past at high speed. The blue seahorse stretched his nose out. His nostrils flapped with excitement. At least *someone* was enjoying himself.

Gilly had made a good start and was already driving Tigershark around the first corner. Lupita was so close that Marnie could feel Eric's whiffling breath on her back. She leaned in to Urchin's bony neck, closed her eyes, and concentrated on not being sick.

Urchin took the second corner so fast that she almost slid off his back. Marnie's hair whipped behind her. She didn't know how Urchin was doing it, but he was closing the gap with Tigershark.

The third corner was even sharper than the second. But Marnie was ready for it this time. She leaned into the turn, her eyes burning as the water rushed past.

Urchin screamed with excitement as they made it around the fourth and final corner. They were neck and neck with Gilly. Urchin swerved around Tigershark's long brown body and pelted for the finish line.

It took every speck of Marnie's concentration to hold on. Marnie and Urchin zoomed to victory, only seconds ahead of Gilly. As Gilly shot over the line, Tigershark's tail smashed into Urchin like a whip. Urchin jumped, almost bucking Marnie off.

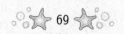

"**SECOND** place means that **YOU LOSE**," said Mr. Marlin, pointing at Gilly and the other competitors. "And **LOSER** team members clean the stables."

Gilly's eyes filled with angry tears. The first years groaned. Seahorse poop was super smelly.

"I'll help," said Marnie, feeling bad for her friends.

Mr. Marlin shrugged. "Suit yourself," he said.

Gilly glared bitterly at Marnie. "I'm not cleaning **ANYTHING**," she snapped.

And with a yank on Tigershark's reins, she galloped away.

Chapter
Eight

At last, Golden Glory Day dawned, bright and clear. The lagoon was still and calm, and the sun filtered through the water, turning everything a lovely pale shade of blue. A little part of Marnie felt excited to get to do cheerleading that day, but she mostly felt as wobbly as a jellyfish. She made herself eat the biggest breakfast she could. She was going to need **ALL** her energy.

Her mom came out of her bedroom and did a little twirl. The peculiar hat on her head looked as if it had been knit out of golden seaweed and was fringed with tiny clinking shells. It was completely ridiculous.

"What do you think?" she asked with excitement. "I made it last night."

"It looks like a plate of seaweed spaghetti," said Aunt Christabel, putting on an enormous pair of rock-crystal earrings. Her long sea-moss scarf floated about her like a beautiful pink cloud. "I feel hungry just looking at you."

"I'll definitely be able to spot you in the crowd, Mom," said Marnie, doing her best to be polite.

"I have to dash, darlings," Christabel said, clipping on Garbo's leash. "What if my team set up the Radio SeaWave booth in the wrong spot? I want a good view of my niece winning the seahorse race so I can give a loud and very unprofessional cheer."

"I thought you didn't like sports, Aunt Christabel," said Marnie.

"I don't." Christabel adjusted her sparkly sunglasses. "But I DO like you."

"Your aunt is impossible," said Marnie's mom as Christabel and Garbo sailed out of the door. "You'd better go, Marnie. You need to get to school. I'll see you after the first event. Good luck!"

Marnie was sure that the water was swirling with an extra sort of energy when she got to registration. For all the problems of Golden Glory Day, she had to admit that it had made life a bit more exciting in Mermaid Lagoon. It also felt very strange to be at school on the weekend.

"I have a plan," Pearl announced.

"Will it get us out of ultra fishball?" Orla asked. She still had a lump on her forehead, but the sparkle was back in her eyes.

"No," said Pearl. "But it WILL make ultra fishball easier."

Marnie peered into the little bag Pearl was holding out. She wrinkled her nose at the smell.

"Flatfish treats," said Pearl triumphantly. "You know how bad-tempered the flatfish were at our last practice? They won't be so grumpy when we've given them these. We might even win a few games."

"But isn't that cheating?" said Marnie doubtfully.

Pearl shook her head. "I checked the rules on Plaicebook. It's totally fine."

When the teachers had ticked everyone's names and the registration scallops had flapped back to the school office, the mermaids lined up in their four teams. Whitecaps were given red seaweed sashes to wear over their shoulders. Billows got blue ones, and Breakers got yellow. Ripples got green sashes, which Gilly immediately called "booger belts."

The mermaids swam out to the sports ground in their teams, grouped nervously together.

As they came around the corner, Marnie got the hazy impression of a large coral reef full of colorful waving flags. From the look of things, the whole of Mermaid Lagoon had turned up for the festivities. She saw her mom's hat right away, but was too nervous to feel embarrassed.

"Wow," said Pearl, looking around. "This is a pretty big deal."

It was bigger than big. It was HUGE. There were merfolk everywhere. Merboys from Atoll Academy had taken the highest seats on the coral stands and were daring each other to do somersaults. Pearl's dad had a stall selling cookies and smoothies, which looked like it was going really well. Music blasted out of the Radio SeaWave booth, which sat between the finishing line for the seahorse race and the driftwood platform where Lady Sealia, her husband Lord Foam, and a few other important guests were sitting. Mr. Marlin had plaited his beard into three braids for the occasion.

Marnie swallowed hard.

"Good morning, Lagooners!"

Christabel's voice boomed across the lagoon bed. Marnie could see Orla's big sister Sheela standing behind Christabel in the Radio SeaWave booth, figuring out the playlist with a pair of shell headphones on her ears while Flip and Sam, the radio producer and sound engineer, fiddled around with the big sea-sponge microphone.

"Golden Glory Day is back and we are ready to **SUSHI ROLL!**" Christabel continued. "Our host for today, Lady Sealia Foam, would like to say a few words of welcome."

Lady Sealia's nose wrinkled disapprovingly. It was clear that she still hadn't forgiven Christabel about Arthur's unexpected appearance at the Clamshell Show.

"Cheerleaders!" Miss Tangle called, beckoning a little hysterically with her tentacles. "Over here! We will perform as soon as Lady Sealia has finished speaking."

The cheerleading stage was beside the ultra fishball court, and it was decorated with colorful seaweed streamers. A few pufferfish floated festively along the front.

"Where are the pom-poms?" Marnie asked, looking around.

Gilly smirked. "You mean **THESE** pom-poms?" she said, waving the snazzy yellow sea anemones at Marnie. "You snooze, you **LOSE**."

"I would like to thank Mr. Marlin for putting together such an exciting program for us today," said Lady Sealia into the microphone. She looked magnificent in a dress covered entirely with pearls.

"I have missed the fun and drama of Golden Glory Day, and I'm delighted that it's back. We may not have the Crown, but we have the *spirit*. I know today will be a great success." Cheers rippled up and down the colorful stands. Miss Tangle lifted her tentacles.

"*Whitecaps surge with sea-foam bright . . .*" began the cheerleading squad. Gilly threw herself into an unscripted somersault with a wave of her pom-poms.

Unfortunately, Lady Sealia hadn't finished yet.

"I'm delighted to say that Miss Haddock is with us today, fresh from her hospital bed," the headmistress continued, glaring at the cheerleaders. "Welcome, Miss Haddock!"

A tiny mermaid with a bandaged tail waved from the coral stands. Miss Haddock's catfish, Cecil, was wearing a large seaweed bow around his neck and didn't look very happy about it.

There was a bit of muttering as the cheerleaders reorganized themselves. The music teacher lifted her tentacles again.

"... *Billows roll with all their might* ..."

"And as Miss Haddock would say," Lady Sealia went on, raising her voice over the song, "it's not the winning that counts—it's the way you say sorry for bumping into your opponents. I am sure you will do her proud, girls, as you remember the spirit of Golden Glory Day. Always be gracious in both victory and defeat!"

There were more cheers. Marnie glanced into the stands and saw Eddy cheerfully blowing a conch trumpet.

"Once more I think," said Miss Tangle.

Marnie and Orla sighed and got back into position.

The music teacher wiped her brow with about five of her tentacles and launched the cheerleading squad for a third time.

"... *Watching Breakers is a treat,*
Ripples are the ones to beat.
Lady Sealia's wins the day,
Lady Sealia's, hip hooray!
Lady Sealia's wins the day,
Lady Sealia's—hip, hip, HOORAY!"

"Well THAT was orca-ward," Orla said when they made it to the end of their routine. "I'm almost looking forward to ultra fishball."

Chapter
Nine

The Ultra Fishball event was a knock-out tournament. Ripples would play Whitecaps first, followed by Breakers against Billows. The winners would then play each other.

"Here," Pearl said, offering the smelly flatfish treats to Marnie and Orla as they joined their teammates. "If the flatfish are in a good mood, they'll do what we want."

"First event of the day: Ultra Fishball!" Christabel said from the Radio SeaWave booth. "Gasp at the speed! Groan at the drama! Cover your eyes at the broken limbs! It's time to get set, GOLDFISH!"

Mr. Marlin put his whelk whistle to his lips and blew.

"And they're OFF—like a bucket of prawns in the sun," said Christabel. "First flatfish throw from Whitecaps. Intercepted by Ripples. Ooh! That was a nasty collision. Ripples throws . . . Or maybe not . . ."

"Pass it, Pearl!" Orla shouted, waving her arms near the flatfish goal. But Mintie Spratt smashed into Pearl like a tsunami and sent her spinning off the court. The crowd roared with excitement.

"SMASH HER BACK!" Mr. Marlin yelled.

"APOLOGIZE!" yelled Miss Haddock, louder than Mr. Marlin.

It seemed like the flatfish was more interested in Pearl's treats than the goal.

"Go on," Pearl shouted, shaking her hand as hard as she could. "The goal's THAT WAY."

Lupita appeared out of nowhere, snatched up the flatfish, and threw it. It rocketed into the net.

"One-nil to Whitecaps!" said Christabel.

"It was the right result," said Pearl as she, Marnie, and Orla watched Whitecaps play Breakers.

"There's nothing right about seventy-six to nothing," said Orla.

"The score *was* a bit high," Pearl admitted. "The flatfish were so *greedy*."

Marnie patted Pearl's arm. "At least we're out of the tournament now," she said. "We just have the Obstacle Relay and the Seahorse Racing to go."

Breakers had beaten Billows in their first-round match, putting them into the final with Whitecaps. The game was moving quickly. The dreamy Zarya Sand-Smith was surprisingly good at guarding the goal, but the combination of Lupita and Cordelia Glitter was unstoppable. When Finnula Gritt and Jaya Wetson were carried off after a head-on collision, Marnie felt more relieved than ever that they had lost.

"Six-all!" said Christabel as a flatfish whirled into the net. "Thrills and gills, fishball was never this exciting when I was at school. And the Whitecaps are off again. This could be the deciding goal . . ."

Marnie rose to the tip of her tail to watch Lupita hurtling down the court. But as Lupita drew back her arm and aimed at the net, Gilly swooped in and chopped hard at Lupita's elbow.

"OW!" Lupita yelled.

"FOUL!" Marnie, Pearl, and Orla shouted as Gilly snatched the fish up.

"SAY SORRY!" Miss Haddock roared.

Now it was Gilly who was racing for her team's goal. The whole of Team Whitecaps was on her tail, but it was no good. The flatfish was already spinning into the net.

"Game, set, and match!" said Christabel.

The crowd erupted into cheers and boos. Team Breakers had won the first event!

"Breakers now have four points," said Christabel when the crowd calmed down. "Whitecaps have three. Billows have two, and Ripples have one. But don't lose heart, my little sea urchins. There are still two events to go!"

One of Marnie's favorite songs, "Tentacular Spectacular," came belting out of the Radio SeaWave booth. But she didn't feel like joining in. The result was unfair, and there was nothing they could do about it.

There was a short break between events. Pearl's dad had sold out of cookies, so Marnie and her friends swam among the food stalls and souvenir booths that had sprung up along the bottom of School Rock, eating sandyfloss instead. Christabel's voice floated over the crowds, teasing and joking and playing upbeat songs.

"You were the best player," said Marnie, offering Lupita a bite of sandyfloss.

"Didn't do us any good though, did it?" sighed

Lupita. She rubbed her sore arm and glared over at Gilly. "I don't care who wins Golden Glory Day now, as long as it's not Gilly Seaflower's team."

"Time for event number two, merfolks," said Christabel. The crowd settled down expectantly. "And it's still anyone's game, with only three points separating Breakers at the top from Ripples at the bottom. Prepare for the Obstacle Relay. Scary spikes! Nasty nets! Murky mud! Terrible tunnels! And of course, the Stinger Surprise. Where will the jellyfish be hiding? Stay tuned, tunafish!"

Lady Sealia frowned and whispered something in Lord Foam's ear. Marnie had a feeling that she hadn't been told about the jellyfish.

As soon as Mr. Marlin blew his whelk whistle, the first group of competitors dived into the race. Orla hadn't practiced the course before, but she still did well for Team Ripples in third position. Pearl had taken her allergy medicine, although it didn't improve her coordination and she cut her tail in three places on the coral spikes.

It's not the winning that counts, Marnie told herself as she darted among the jagged edges of the coral spikes. She just wanted to do her best.

She focused hard and plunged under the first seaweed net like an eel. The net was as slimy as ever, but she made it to the other side in record time. A flick of her tail this way, a pull of her arms that way—and she was through. The mud was next. Marnie drove through the gloop with Gilly right behind her.

Muddy water swirled around Marnie as she raced for the mouth of the tunnel and threw herself into the darkness. She focused on the opening at the far end and swam as hard as she could.

There was a sudden scream behind her.

"HELP!"

Marnie paused. She couldn't ignore a scream like that.

"Gilly?" she called into the darkness.

Gilly screamed again. "Help! Help, Marnie!"

The jellyfish? Again? Marnie couldn't believe Gilly could be so unlucky. But she didn't hesitate. Turning around, she swam back, moving her arms gently through the gloom, trying to find her way.

"Gilly?" she called. "Are you OK? I'll get help, hold on . . ."

She was blinded by a sudden flash of light. The glowing jellyfish was right in front of her.

It was huge.

Its tentacles glimmered as they brushed against Marnie's arms. Marnie felt a terrible bolt of pain—and then everything went black.

Chapter Ten

Opening her eyes, Marnie stared at the dirty old chandelier above her. She was in the First Aid Cave.

"What happened?" she asked groggily.

Marnie's mom was holding her hand. Her seaweed hat had slipped sideways. "You're awake! Oh Marnie, are you OK?"

Marnie had a sudden memory of the glowing jellyfish wrapping its tentacles around her. "I don't know," she said honestly.

She felt a tickling sensation around her chin. Garbo was flitting anxiously around her head. She pet the little fish's golden scales and winced as pain shot down her arm.

"It's outrageous to put a jellyfish into a school obstacle course," her mom said, fiercely. "I'm going to have strong words with Lady Sealia."

"Go on then, Daffy," Christabel said, floating over to Marnie's bed. "Garbo and I will stay with Marnie."

Marnie's mom straightened her hat and left, muttering about PE teachers with biceps bigger than their brains. Marnie struggled to sit up. It was difficult because her arms and tummy were wrapped in seaweed bandages.

"What happened to Gilly?" she asked her aunt.

"The blonde girl?" said Christabel in surprise. "She looked fine to me."

"But she screamed . . ." Marnie trailed off. What exactly had happened in that tunnel?

"With excitement, probably," said Christabel. "Her team won the relay."

Marnie tried to make sense of this. Gilly had definitely screamed. She'd heard it, loud and clear. But then . . . the jellyfish . . . A cold feeling settled in her stomach. Had Gilly lured her into the jellyfish on *purpose*?

Marnie stopped trying to figure it out, and flopped back on her pillow. "Why are you here, Aunt Christabel? You're supposed to be doing the Radio SeaWave broadcast."

"I left Sheela in charge," said Christabel. "She has an excellent line in clam jokes. Sheela's been working for me for a while now, and this seemed like a golden oppor-tuna-ty to give her a crack at the limelight. I couldn't tell jokes and play songs with you lying in the First Aid Cave, could I? You're my favorite niece."

"I'm your only niece," Marnie pointed out.

Christabel took Marnie's hand. "You gave us a terrible fright when you came floating out of the tunnel with

your eyes closed and your body covered in jellyfish stings," she said. "Don't do it again."

"I'll try not to," Marnie said.

Christabel gazed up at the old chandelier. "The last time I was in this place was just before the old Golden Glory Day," she said. "The whole school competed back then, even those of us at the top of the school."

"Were you sick?" Marnie asked.

"In a way," Christabel said. She sighed. "Seasickness stinks, but lovesickness is worse."

Marnie forgot her injuries.

"Was it Arthur?" she said. "What happened?"

Christabel had a faraway look in her eyes. "We had been meeting secretly at the East Lagoon Rocks for a few weeks. We wanted to be together, but it was impossible. Then I had a bright idea. I decided to steal the Golden Glory Crown."

Marnie gasped. Christabel had stolen the Crown? But why?

Then, suddenly, she realized.

"The *wish*!" she said. "You took the Crown to make a wish, didn't you?"

"I did," her aunt admitted. "But nothing happened. No flash of magic, no sparkles in the water." Garbo nibbled gently on her ear. "The wish only worked for the winner of Golden Glory Day."

"So you didn't win?" Marnie asked.

Christabel made a face. "I didn't compete at all! I stole the Crown from Lady Sealia's study the night before, put it on, and wished that Arthur and I could be together forever. When the wish didn't work, I was furious. And . . . I hid the Crown. The next day, when Lady Sealia found the Crown was missing, she canceled the whole event. I felt guilty about it for a while, but then

Golden Glory Day faded from everyone's memories and it didn't seem important anymore. Until Daffy started talking about it the other day, I hadn't thought about the Crown for years." She frowned. "Or felt guilty about it."

Marnie had a sudden rush of excitement. This was the answer to the mystery. And her aunt held the key!

"Where did you hide it?" she asked eagerly.

There was a swirl of water. Sam, Christabel's green-bearded sound engineer, swam into the First Aid Cave.

"You all right, Marnie?" he said. "Sorry Christabel, but we need you back at the booth. Sheela's doing great, but she's running out of clam jokes and the crowd is getting restless."

"Where is the Crown, Aunt Christabel?" Marnie repeated.

Garbo darted among the pink folds of Christabel's floating sea-moss scarf as she leaned down to whisper something in Marnie's ear.

"*Amid the gloom, amid the green, find the gold and meet the Queen.*" She patted Marnie's cheek. "Find it for me, Marnie. It's time I gave it back."

And then her aunt was gone.

Marnie had never felt more awake in her life. She tried to get out of bed. Her jellyfish stings twinged underneath her bandages, but she ignored them. The Crown was gold, she imagined, and the Queen was probably Maretta . . . but what about the rest? The gloom, and the green?

The last time I was in this place was just before the old Golden Glory Day. Christabel said she hadn't been sick. So why had she been in the First Aid Cave at all?

"To hide the Crown," Marnie said out loud. It must be hidden in here. It *must* be.

She looked around the rocky little room. The shelves were packed with medicine bottles. There was nothing under her bed. There was nowhere to hide something as bulky as a crown.

"Get back in your bed!" Nurse Nurse-Shark swam back into the cave. "At once!"

Marnie reluctantly lay down again. The old chandelier jingled high above her. And then . . . Then . . .

A flash of gold.

"Nurse?" said Marnie. "Please may I have something to drink? I'm very thirsty."

Marnie waited until the nurse shark's large tail had disappeared around the corner to fetch some sea anemone juice. Then she pushed up from her bed and swam to the ceiling.

And there, up on the gloomy ceiling, tucked in among the green branches of the chandelier, was a large golden crown.

The Last Chapter

Marnie carefully lifted the Golden Glory Crown from its hiding place. Even after all the years it had spent tucked into the grubby chandelier, the glitter of gold and jewels was dazzling. She held her breath as she looked at the twisting branches of coral, the tiny seed pearls, and the enormous rock crystal at its heart. It was magnificent.

Through the fog of her thoughts, Marnie heard the distant roar of the crowd. Golden Glory Day was nearly over. If Gilly *had* lured her into the jellyfish in order to win, then Gilly was a cheater. And a cheater couldn't win Golden Glory Day.

There wasn't a moment to lose. Marnie had to set things right.

As she barreled out of the First Aid Cave, she almost knocked the sea anemone juice out of the nurse shark's grasp.

"What are you doing?" called Nurse Nurse-Shark anxiously. "You should be in bed! Come back! Come back at once!"

Marnie yanked off her bandages, pushed away the pain of her jellyfish stings and swam as hard as she could, clutching the Golden Glory Crown to her chest. As she hurtled out of School Rock and around the corner, she was nearly flattened by a thundering line of seahorses.

The race was almost over. Gilly was in the lead, riding Tigershark like a sea dragon was on her tail.

That could have been me, Marnie thought a little wistfully.

Eric and Sandy were nearby. A long way behind was Pearl, riding the mild-mannered Andrew. The crowd roared.

As soon as the coast was clear, Marnie swam toward the driftwood stage, where Lady Sealia and her guests were sitting. She noticed that Urchin had climbed into the radio booth and was nuzzling Christabel's neck.

"YOU'RE STODGIER THAN LAST WEEK'S KELP CASSEROLE!" Mr. Marlin roared, even though the thundering riders couldn't hear him. "MOVE IT!"

"And here they come!" Christabel said over the microphone. "It's Gilly Seaflower on Tigershark in the lead. Lupita Barracuda on Eric and Mabel Anemone on Sandy are doing their best to catch up, but it's no good. And somewhere in the distance, we have Pearl Cockle on Andrew. Of course, Andrew is completely hopeless, but he's a charming animal and Pearl Cockle is doing her best. Get *off*, Urchin!

Your fins are tickling me. Tigershark is almost there . . .
Eric is swimming up on the inside—but Tigershark
wins it!"

"Brea**KERS!**" shouted Gilly's team, waving their
yellow sashes in the air like flags as Tigershark shot
over the finishing line. "Brea**KERS!** Brea**KERS!**"

Radio SeaWave played a blast of "In It to Fin It," a
classic pop track with a catchy beat.

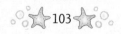

"And at the end of an eventful day," Christabel said as the song played out, "Ripples have three points. Billows have six. Whitecaps have nine points. And Breakers score a whopping twelve. STOP NIBBLING MY EARS, URCHIN!"

"BreaKERS! BreaKERS!" the winning team shouted.

Lady Sealia's voice rang through the crowd. "I am delighted to announce that Team Breakers have won," she said. "Congratulations. I would like to invite our, ah, *special guest* Christabel Blue to shake hands with our lucky winners."

The crowd cheered. Lady Sealia watched frostily as Christabel came out of the Radio SeaWave booth with Urchin beside her chewing on her pink scarf. Garbo flitted around Urchin's tail, giving him jealous little nips.

"I won!" Gilly cheered.

"Your *team* won," Lady Sealia corrected.

Marnie's stings were hurting really badly now.

"Lady Sealia!" she gasped, waving the Crown. "Wait!"

The crowd fell silent. Then the whispers began.

"Is that . . ."

"It can't be . . ."

"Wherever did she . . ."

"*My daughter has the Golden Glory Crown!*" Marnie's mom gasped, clutching her seaweed hat.

Lady Sealia took the Crown from Marnie's hands and stared at the gold and jewels and twisting coral branches. Dilys opened one sleepy eye and sniffed it.

"It's a miracle," Lady Sealia gasped, putting a hand to her heart.

"You found it!" said Orla, swooshing up to give Marnie a hug. "Was it in Lady Sealia's office like I said?"

"Don't squeeze me," Marnie begged. "My jellyfish stings hurt."

"Oops," said Orla, quickly letting go. "Sorry. Everyone's saying Gilly pushed you into the jellyfish. Is it true?"

"She didn't . . . push me," said Marnie, still panting hard. "But I think . . . she pretended she was hurt, so I went back to help her. That's when I was stung."

Orla whistled. "You turned around to help Gilly Seaflower? You are SO weird."

The crowd was still cheering the amazing reappearance of the Crown.

"Make a wish!" someone shouted.

The crowd took up the chant. "Make a wish, make a wish, MAKE A WISH!"

Lady Sealia reluctantly gave the Crown to Christabel to make the presentation.

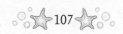

Christabel stroked the Crown's sparkling coral branches. Marnie guessed that her aunt was thinking of Arthur, and the wish she'd tried to make all those years ago.

Looking up, Christabel smiled at the mermaids of Team Breakers. "Which one of you is going to make a wish for your team?" she asked.

"It's not up to them," said Gilly loudly. "It's up to ME. I did all the work."

She snatched the Crown from Christabel and rammed it on her head. "I wish that I could be the BEST in EVERYTHING and for ALL TIME!" she shouted.

But nothing happened. Not a fizz, or a spark, or a flash. The other mermaids in Team Breakers frowned and muttered among themselves.

Gilly pouted. "This thing doesn't work," she said, taking it off again.

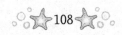

"That's because you're not the true winner, Gilly," said Marnie, who had finally got her breath back. "You hit Lupita in ultra fishball, and you pretended you were hurt in the tunnel so that I would turn back and get stung. And then I couldn't ride in the seahorse race so you could win on Tigershark. You're a CHEATER. And the Golden Glory Crown doesn't like cheaters!"

Dilys gave a snoozy-sounding growl. Eddy blew his conch trumpet and was loudly shushed.

Lady Sealia seemed to grow very tall and fierce. "Is this true, Gilly?" she asked.

"Yes!" Orla shouted.

"Every word!" Lupita cried.

Suddenly everyone was pointing at Gilly.

"She took all the cheerleading pom-poms for herself!" complained Marina Bailey.

"She ate my sandyfloss without asking!" said Finnula Gritt.

Gilly's lip wobbled. "Mr. Marlin said that winning was the only thing that mattered. He said no one cared about how you won, as long as you got the prize."

Mr. Marlin cleared his throat. "That's not *quite* what I said—"

"He said no one remembered you if you came in second," Gilly wailed.

"I did say that," Mr. Marlin admitted. "Because it's true. But—"

"I . . . I don't want to be forgotten!" Gilly wept.

Lady Sealia glared at the burly PE teacher. "We do not encourage winning at all costs at this school," she said. "And whatever were you thinking, introducing a dangerous jellyfish to a school event? You are in a GREAT deal of trouble, Mr. Marlin."

"APOLOGIZE!" shouted Miss Haddock shrilly.

There was a sudden movement in Lady Sealia's arms. Remarkably, Dilys had opened BOTH her eyes— at the same time. To everyone's astonishment, the little dogfish suddenly darted away from Lady Sealia with her narrow jaws open wide . . . and sank her sharp little shark teeth into Mr. Marlin's scaly bottom.

"OW!" roared Mr. Marlin. "Get this animal off me! I'll report you . . . OOH! OW!"

The crowd roared with laughter as Dilys darted around Mr. Marlin, nipping away at his arms, and his tail and nose. Miss Haddock's catfish, Cecil, wriggled out of his seaweed bow and swam over to pull Mr. Marlin's beard.

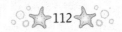

"Ooh!" squealed the PE teacher. "**YOW!**"

"Poor Mr. Marlin," Marnie said, feeling sorry for their teacher.

Orla rolled her eyes. "I will **NEVER** understand you."

"As a result of Gilly Seaflower's actions," Lady Sealia said, "I can no longer award the Crown to Team Breakers. Would a representative of Team Whitecaps please come up and accept the prize instead?"

Team Breakers groaned. Gilly sobbed harder. Team Whitecaps clustered together for a moment, and then started waving their red sashes in the air. Lots of arms pushed Lupita to the front of the crowd. With a kick of her sparkling tail, Lupita swam up to the stage.

"Thank you everyone," Lupita said with a wave. "I'm really glad that Team Whitecaps won, obviously. But everyone played really well. It's been an awesome day."

"Are you going to make a wish on behalf of Team Whitecaps?" Christabel asked as she presented Lupita with the glittering Crown.

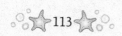

"We talked about it." Lupita glanced at her teammates. "And we decided to give the wish to someone else. Is that allowed?"

The crowd murmured in surprise.

Christabel tucked Garbo into the folds of her pink scarf. "I have no idea," she said. "But I can tell you from experience that the Crown loves fair play. So it's worth a try."

Lupita grinned. "Then on behalf of Team Whitecaps, I want to give the wish to Marnie Blue."

Marnie gaped. "What?" she stammered.

"We only won because of you," Lupita pointed out. "So we figured that maybe you'd like the wish."

Marnie felt like she was in a dream. There was the sound of cheering. Hands and fins pushed her gently up to the stage, and then suddenly she was looking into her aunt's shining violet eyes and the Crown was in her hands.

"I don't know what to say," she croaked.

"I'll give you a clue," said Aunt Christabel with her famously warm smile. "It starts like this: 'I wish . . .'"

Tail polish? Marnie thought wildly. *New pearl earrings?*

And then it came to her. She put the Crown on her head.

"I wish for true happiness for my Aunt Christabel," she said.

As she spoke, she had a sudden vision of a big wedding for Christabel and Arthur. There would be amazing food like barnacle buns and limpet lollipops, and there would be traditional wave dancing, and she would be a tidesmaid. It would be AMAZING!

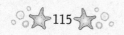

There was a loud fizzing. Balls of bright blue light swirled around Marnie's head. The crowd drew back in awe as a tall, glowing mermaid appeared in the water.

"Interesting wish," Queen Maretta said. The crown on her head was even sparklier than Marnie's, and she held a twisting coral scepter between her long fingers. "It seems so simple. But happiness is a slippery fish and swims where it wants."

Marnie felt dizzy gazing into the fabled Mermaid Queen's glowing eyes.

"Your wish, Marnie Blue, is granted," the queen said. "But it may not turn out quite the way you expect."

And with a spin of her coral scepter, the queen vanished in a bubble of water.

The crowd erupted into cheers. Aunt Christabel swept Marnie into a hug, and Marnie didn't even notice her jellyfish stings. Marnie's mom threw her hat in the air, where it was eaten by a passing manatee.

Everything was perfect.

"Hi Marnie!" came a voice. Pearl was finally crossing the finishing line on Andrew.

"Are you feeling better now?" Pearl asked, sliding off Andrew's back. "I had to do the race on Andrew when you didn't come back. I didn't do very well, I'm afraid, but I did see a giant spotted sailfish behind School Rock, which was *off the reef*!"

She gazed at the cheering crowd, and the crown on Marnie's head, and the pet fish chasing Mr. Marlin, and the sniffing Gilly, and the huge smile on Christabel Blue's face.

"What did I miss?!" she asked.

About the Author

Lucy Courtenay has worked on a number of series for young readers, as well as books for young adults. When not writing, she enjoys singing, reading, and traveling. She lives in Farnham, England, with her husband, her two sons, and a cat named Crumbles.

About the Illustrator

Sheena Dempsey is a children's book illustrator and author from Cork, Ireland, who was shortlisted for the Sainsbury's Book Award. She lives in London with her partner, Mick, and her retired racing greyhound, Sandy.